Bearsted Library
The Green
Bearsted
Tel: Maidstone 739774

28. MAR 08   14. FEB 09
13 OCT 2009
19. APR 08

30. MAY 08
27. JUN 08
02. AUG 08
28. SEP 08.

M41

2 1 APR 2011   2 5 JUN 2016
                    1 5 NOV 2016
- 9 FEB 2012
- 7 AUG 2012
2 2 SEP 2012   1 1 DEC 2018
1 6 FEB 2010
- 6 NOV 2012
9th March WITHDRAWN
2 0 JUL 2010
- 1 JUN 2013   - 3 SEP 2019
E 4 SEP 2014
2 0 AUG 2010
2 4 OCT 2015
- 9 OCT 2010   1 1 MAR 2016

Please return on or before the latest date above.
You can renew online at *www.kent.gov.uk/libs*
or by telephone 08458 247 200

CUSTOMER SERVICE EXCELLENCE **Libraries & Archives**

00884\DTP\RN\07.07   LIB 7

C153243372

D1412944

First published in 2007 by
Franklin Watts
338 Euston Road
London
NW1 3BH

Franklin Watts Australia
Level 17/207 Kent Street
Sydney
NSW 2000

Text © Barrie Wade 2007
Illustration © O'Kif 2007

The rights of Barrie Wade to be identified as the author
and O'Kif as the illustrator of this Work have
been asserted in accordance with the Copyright, Designs
and Patents Act, 1988.

All rights reserved. No part of this publication may be
reproduced, stored in a retrieval system, or transmitted
in any form or by any means, electronic, mechanical,
photocopy, recording or otherwise, without the prior
written permission of the copyright owner.

A CIP catalogue record for this book is available
from the British Library.

ISBN 978 0 7496 7077 1 (hbk)
ISBN 978 0 7496 7421 2 (pbk)

Series Editor: Melanie Palmer
Series Advisor: Dr Barrie Wade
Series Designer: Peter Scoulding

Printed in China

Franklin Watts is a division of Hachette Children's Books.

KENT
LIBRARIES & ARCHIVES

C153243372

The
Emperor's
New Clothes

by Barrie Wade and O'Kif

W

FRANKLIN WATTS

LONDON•SYDNEY

Once there lived a vain Emperor
who loved to show off
in new clothes.

One day, two weavers came to his palace. "We can weave you the best robes in the world," said one.

"Our beautiful cloth is so fine that stupid people cannot even see it!" said the other.

"Fantastic," said the Emperor.
"There is a procession next week
and I want to wear the grandest
robes ever made."

8

The vain Emperor gave the weavers
a bag of gold and a room in the
palace. The cheating weavers
pretended to work.

Everyone wondered what the
Emperor would wear for the
royal procession.

"The weavers are making a special cloth. It is so fine that stupid people cannot see it!" said the royal maid.

Royal
procession
Next
week

The Emperor sent his Prime
Minister to see the weavers.
"Look at the splendid colours!"
said one weaver.

"Look at the beautiful pattern!"
said the other. The Prime Minister
could not see anything, but he did
not want to seem stupid.

"What splendid colours! What a beautiful pattern!" he reported to the Emperor.

So the Emperor sent the weavers
another bag of gold.

Later, the Emperor sent his Chancellor to see how the weavers were getting on.

"Look at the lovely colours! Look at the marvellous pattern!" said the cheating weavers.

The Chancellor had not seen
anything either, but he did not
want to admit he was stupid.

"What lovely colours! What a
marvellous pattern!" he reported
to the Emperor. The Emperor gave
the weavers another bag of gold.

At last the weavers carried the finished cloth to the Emperor.

"Look at the marvellous pattern!"
said the Chancellor.

"Look at the splendid colours!"
said the Prime Minister.

The Emperor looked, but he could
not see anything. However, he
did not want to seem stupid.
"How magnificent!" he said.

The procession was the next day.
The cheating weavers pretended to
cut and sew the cloth into robes.

23

At last they cried: "The Emperor's new robes are ready."

The Emperor took off his clothes
and the weavers pretended to dress
him in his new robes.

"A perfect fit!" all his ministers
cried. They could not see anything,
but nobody wanted to seem stupid.

The cheating weavers quickly
left with their gold.

The Emperor walked in the procession with his ministers. In the streets, the people cheered.

"What a magnificent robe!" they cried. They could not see anything either, but nobody wanted to appear stupid.

Suddenly a child pointed, yelling:
"The Emperor has got nothing on!"
"That's right!" the people shouted.
"He's got nothing on!"

Everyone laughed. The vain Emperor blushed and felt very, very stupid.

Hopscotch has been specially designed to fit the requirements of the National Literacy Strategy. It offers real books by top authors and illustrators for children developing their reading skills. There are 43 Hopscotch stories to choose from:

Marvin, the Blue Pig
ISBN 978 0 7496 4619 6

Plip and Plop
ISBN 978 0 7496 4620 2

The Queen's Dragon
ISBN 978 0 7496 4618 9

Flora McQuack
ISBN 978 0 7496 4621 9

Willie the Whale
ISBN 978 0 7496 4623 3

Naughty Nancy
ISBN 978 0 7496 4622 6

Run!
ISBN 978 0 7496 4705 6

The Playground Snake
ISBN 978 0 7496 4706 3

"Sausages!"
ISBN 978 0 7496 4707 0

The Truth about Hansel and Gretel
ISBN 978 0 7496 4708 7

Pippin's Big Jump
ISBN 978 0 7496 4710 0

Whose Birthday Is It?
ISBN 978 0 7496 4709 4

The Princess and the Frog
ISBN 978 0 7496 5129 9

Flynn Flies High
ISBN 978 0 7496 5130 5

Clever Cat
ISBN 978 0 7496 5131 2

Moo!
ISBN 978 0 7496 5332 3

Izzie's Idea
ISBN 978 0 7496 5334 7

Roly-poly Rice Ball
ISBN 978 0 7496 5333 0

I Can't Stand It!
ISBN 978 0 7496 5765 9

Cockerel's Big Egg
ISBN 978 0 7496 5767 3

How to Teach a Dragon Manners
ISBN 978 0 7496 5873 1

The Truth about those Billy Goats
ISBN 978 0 7496 5766 6

Marlowe's Mum and the Tree House
ISBN 978 0 7496 5874 8

Bear in Town
ISBN 978 0 7496 5875 5

The Best Den Ever
ISBN 978 0 7496 5876 2

ADVENTURE STORIES

Aladdin and the Lamp
ISBN 978 0 7496 6678 1 *
ISBN 978 0 7496 6692 7

Blackbeard the Pirate
ISBN 978 0 7496 6676 7 *
ISBN 978 0 7496 6690 3

George and the Dragon
ISBN 978 0 7496 6677 4 *
ISBN 978 0 7496 6691 0

Jack the Giant-Killer
ISBN 978 0 7496 6680 4 *
ISBN 978 0 7496 6693 4

TALES OF KING ARTHUR

1. The Sword in the Stone
ISBN 978 0 7496 6681 1 *
ISBN 978 0 7496 6694 1

2. Arthur the King
ISBN 978 0 7496 6683 5 *
ISBN 978 0 7496 6695 8

3. The Round Table
ISBN 978 0 7496 6684 2 *
ISBN 978 0 7496 6697 2

4. Sir Lancelot and the Ice Castle
ISBN 978 0 7496 6685 9 *
ISBN 978 0 7496 6698 9

TALES OF ROBIN HOOD

Robin and the Knight
ISBN 978 0 7496 6686 6 *
ISBN 978 0 7496 6699 6

Robin and the Monk
ISBN 978 0 7496 6687 3 *
ISBN 978 0 7496 6700 9

Robin and the Friar
ISBN 978 0 7496 6688 0 *
ISBN 978 0 7496 6702 3

Robin and the Silver Arrow
ISBN 978 0 7496 6689 7 *
ISBN 978 0 7496 6703 0

FAIRY TALES

The Emperor's New Clothes
ISBN 978 0 7496 7077 1 *
ISBN 978 0 7496 7421 2

Cinderella
ISBN 978 0 7496 7073 3 *
ISBN 978 0 7496 7417 5

Snow White
ISBN 978 0 7496 7074 0 *
ISBN 978 0 7496 7418 2

Jack and the Beanstalk
ISBN 978 0 7496 7078 8 *
ISBN 978 0 7496 7422 9

The Three Billy Goats Gruff
ISBN 978 0 7496 7076 4 *
ISBN 978 0 7496 7420 5

The Pied Piper of Hamelin
ISBN 978 0 7496 7075 7 *
ISBN 978 0 7496 7419 9

* hardback